My Faraway Grandma:

A promise of love

by

Stella Lawton

This book belongs to

.

FOR

SERENA

You are always in
my thoughts.

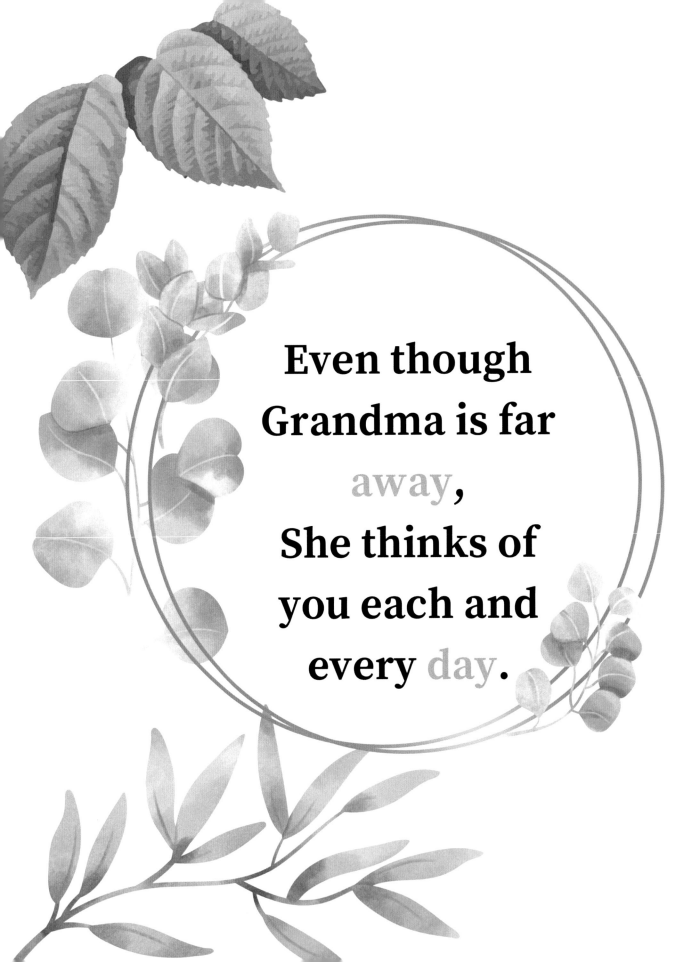

Even though Grandma is far away,
She thinks of you each and every day.

From morning's first light until evening's last glow, Grandma's thinking of you; this is something you should know.

She thinks of your smile, your giggle, and your coos.
and all the wonderful things that you do.

She thinks of the stories she'll share with you.

and all the adventures you'll have when you're two.

Her love for you is like
a beautiful flower.
that blooms in her
heart every minute,
every hour.

So when you look
up at the bright
blue sky,
Or watch a
butterfly flutter by,

Always remember this one simple truth, even though Grandma is far away.

She loves you more and more every day.

So when you
wake up to a
bright new
day,
Remember,
Grandma's love
is here to stay.

In her heart, you'll always find:
A love that's pure and endlessly kind.

Grandma's loves you more than the sun up high,
and the fluffy clouds in the sky.

She loves you
more with each
passing day,
in every single
little way.

In her heart,
you're never far.
For love knows no
distance, no
matter where you
are.

She dreams of the day
when she'll hold you
tight,
and shower you with
kisses and love all
through the day and
night.
Until then, remember this
one simple truth:
Grandma loves you more
than words can say,
more than there are stars
in the Milky Way.

There is only one last
thing I can say.
Even though
Grandma's far away,
She thinks of you
each and every day.

And when we're finally
reunited at last,
We'll make memories
that will never be
surpassed.

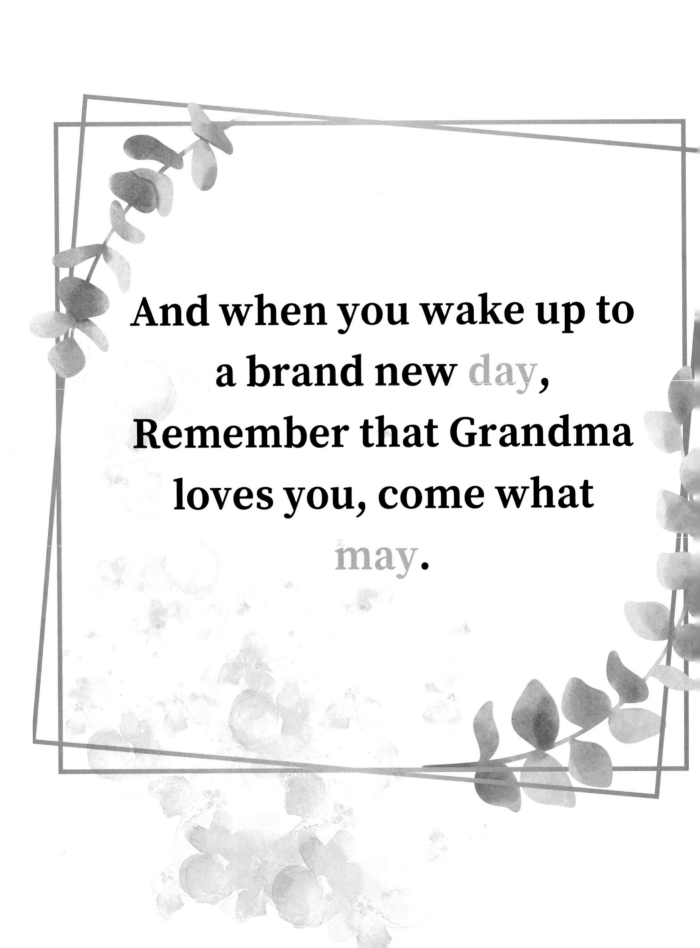

And when you wake up to a brand new day, Remember that Grandma loves you, come what may.

Made in the USA
Las Vegas, NV
02 December 2024

13199423R00017